Robin Hood

RETOLD BY
BOB BLAISDELL

Illustrated by Thea Kliros

Dover Publications, Inc.
New York

Bibliographical Note

Robin Hood is a new work, first published by Dover Publications, Inc., in 1994.

Library of Congress Cataloging-in-Publication Data

Blaisdell, Bob.
    Robin Hood / retold by Bob Blaisdell ; illustrated by Thea Kliros.
        p.   cm. — (Dover children's thrift series)
    Summary: Recounts the life and adventures of Robin Hood, who, with his band of followers, lived in Sherwood Forest as an outlaw dedicated to fighting tyranny.
    ISBN 0-486-27573-6 (pbk.)
    1. Robin Hood (Legendary character)—Legends. [1. Robin Hood (Legendary character) 2. Folklore—England.] I. Robin Hood (Legend). English. II. Kliros, Thea, ill. III. Title. IV. Series.
PZ8.1.B5826Ro   1994
398.22—dc20
[E]   94-9381
                                                                  CIP
                                                                   AC

Manufactured in the United States of America
Dover Publications, Inc., 31 East 2nd Street, Mineola, N.Y. 11501

Note

ROBIN HOOD is one of the great folk figures in English tradition. Our information about his legend comes from brief old poems in which single adventures are told. Part of the tradition was also created much later by Sir Walter Scott in his novel *Ivanhoe*. In the nineteenth and twentieth centuries there have been many books telling a continuous story about Robin Hood (and, of course, a number of very successful movies), but there is no one accepted unified version; every complete story is an individual author's imaginative regrouping of the separate elements of the legend.

For the present volume Robert Blaisdell has written a new text based closely on authentic old material. He does not attempt to narrate all the incidents that have been connected with Robin Hood, but concentrates on the most familiar and basic ones, making sure that all the favorite characters are included.

Contents

List of Illustrations

Robin Hood and Little John

ROBIN HOOD was born long, long ago in Locksley town, not far from Nottingham. As a boy Robin worked in Sherwood Forest with his father, a forester who planted and nursed the trees in the King's woodlands. Robin's father was an expert with the bow and arrow, and Robin learned to shoot a bow from him. Robin's mother was the niece of a knight, Sir Jervey. Her brother was Gamwell, a squire of famous degree, of Great Gamwell Hall. Robin was sixteen when his parents died of an illness. So unhappy was he that he wandered the forest for several days. Finally he grew so hungry he shot his bow and killed a deer.

In Sherwood Forest all the deer belonged to the King and, unluckily for young Robin, the Sheriff of Nottingham, a young man then himself, captured and arrested him for the killing of that deer and of many others. Robin pleaded innocent to the killing of all but the one, saying that he had been lost and hungry, grieving for his parents. Nevertheless, the Sheriff sentenced Robin to death by hanging.

At the last moment a band of men, bold thieves and hunters who lived in a lodge in the forest, rescued Robin from the scaffold. He then joined them in their adventures and, thanks to his wits and skill in archery, soon became their leader.

When Robin Hood was about twenty years old, he met Little John. Though called "Little," his limbs were large and his height was seven feet, and wherever he went, people quaked in their shoes.

The day they met, Robin said to his jolly men, "Wait here in this grove and listen for my signal. I shall search the forest for deer to shoot or a rich man to rob."

When he came to a small stream, he happened to meet an enormous young stranger halfway across the narrow footbridge. Neither man would make way for the other, and so they had a standstill. Robin Hood, who had a temper, said, "I'll show you," and drew an arrow to his bow.

The black-bearded stranger answered, his voice a growl, "I'll thrash you well, my puny man, if you dare to twitch your bowstring."

"You donkey!" said Robin. "If I bend my bow at you, in an instant I can send an arrow through your heart."

"You are a coward," the stranger replied.

"You have a bow with arrows to shoot at me, while I have nothing but a staff in my hand."

"A coward!" said Robin, who had never been addressed so. "Not I! I'll set down my bow and fetch myself a staff."

Robin Hood went back along his path and found a staff of oak, and returned to his place on the bridge. "I'm ready, bold man. Look at my staff, and here on this bridge, we'll have a contest. Whoever falls in, the other shall win, and so by that we'll settle this."

"I agree," said the stranger. "I'm happy to compete."

They fell into battle and swung their strong staffs. At first Robin gave the stranger a bang so hard it made the big man's bones ring. The staggered stranger said, "I'll give as good as I got."

So to it again they went, their staffs in a whirl, and the giant of a man gave Robin such a crack on the skull that Robin saw red. Then Robin Hood, enraged, went at it more fiercely, and struck at the stranger harder. The stranger laughed at Robin's fury. Robin, too mad to see straight, because this man seemed to mock him, lost his balance, was struck by the stranger's powerful staff, and tumbled into the stream.

"I ask you, friend," laughed the stranger, "where are you now?"

They fell into battle and swung their strong staffs.

"I see I'm in the stream," said Robin, his temper now cooled in the cold, rushing stream. "I must acknowledge your strength. I shall no longer fight you—you have won."

Robin waded up onto the bank, and then blew his horn. His men came, clothed in green, to the spot.

"What's the matter?" said Midge the miller's son. "Good master, you're wet to the skin."

"This man knocked me in," said Robin.

"We'll get him for that," said Will Stutely.

Robin cried out, "You will find he's tough." Will took a swing at the stranger, but soon found himself taking a bath in the stream. Midge the miller's son tried to outsmart the big stranger, but the stranger's great strength was smarter than Midge's smarts. Midge, too, was soon sitting in the stream.

"Who else?" cried the stranger.

Now Robin said, "No one will attack you again, my friend. But why not join us and wear our cloak of green? I'll teach you how to use the bow and arrow to shoot at fat deer."

"I like deer," said the stranger. "But where do you find deer that don't belong to the King?"

"Right here in my forest," said Robin Hood. "The deer belong to the forest, and the forest belongs to those who live in it. I and my men live here, and these are our deer."

"And what about the Sheriff of Notting-ham?" asked the stranger. "He does not see it the way you do. He serves the King and sets traps and hangs those who hunt the King's deer."

"The Sheriff is our foe, and the deer are ours to eat, as they are any honest man's. The deer belonged to the forest before they belonged to any king. We defend the rights of poor, hungry men to hunt for their food. The King will have to bear this. Please join us."

"I'll join you," said the stranger. "I swear I'll serve you faithfully. I'm a poor man, too. My name is John Little."

"His name should be changed," said Midge. "It's backwards, I think." At the feast which then followed, Robin and the men, as a joke, rechristened him Little John.

"We live here like squires," Robin told him. "We feast on good meat, wine and ale. We have the forest at our command. You are so grand and fine a fellow, you shall be my right-hand man."

"Very good," replied Little John. "And you shall be my lord."

Sir Richard and His Castle

ONE AFTERNOON Little John said to Robin Hood, "Master, it's about time you ate. It would do you good."

Robin Hood answered, "I do not feel like eating today, unless I have some rich and worthy knight as my guest, a man who might pay us for a feast."

"Tell us, then," said Little John, "where to go and whom to rob."

"Of course you must not rob any poor men, nor any good men that are squires. But rich churchmen, nobles and knights are fair game," said Robin Hood. "Take your good bow in your hand, Little John, and let Midge and Will Stutely go with you. Wait for our unknown guest, be he an earl, baron, bishop or knight, and bring him here to me."

Little John led the men and waited by the highway, till finally riding from the town there came a sad and grieving knight. Little John stepped out into the highway and went down on one knee. "Welcome, sir knight," politely said Little John. "Welcome to Sherwood

7

Forest. My master is waiting for you to come to dinner."

"Who is your master?" asked the knight.

Little John said, "Robin Hood."

"I have heard good things of Robin Hood. I agree to go with you, my friends." Even so, the knight was sad as he followed Little John, Midge and Will. There was some trouble on his mind that Little John could not discover. They brought him to the lodge door where Robin and all the men lived. When Robin saw him, he too went down on his knee. "Welcome, sir knight, you are welcome to our home. I have been waiting to serve you dinner."

The knight answered, "Thank you, Robin, and all your good men."

They washed and then sat down together to dine. They had bread and wine, and good deer steaks, swans, pheasants and waterfowl.

"Did you enjoy your meal?" asked Robin.

"Thank you," said the knight. "Such a dinner I have not had in many a year. If I ever come to your country again, Robin, I shall prepare for you a dinner as splendid as this you made me."

"Whenever I serve a dinner, sir knight, I am never so greedy as to eat it alone. Tell me your name now. But I must tell you, I expect you to pay for this dinner. Our rule here is that the rich must pay."

"My name is Sir Richard," said the sad knight, "but I am ashamed to say that I have no more than ten pennies."

"If you have no more than ten, I will not charge you a penny. And if you have need of any money, I shall lend it to you," said Robin Hood. "Little John, please look and see if what the knight says is so."

Little John looked through the knight's moneybox, and then went to his master. "It is true," he said.

"How is it," said Robin to the knight, "that you have lost your riches?"

"I had a son, good Robin, who jousted with a knight. When in that fight my son was killed, I paid out money to find his slayer, one Guy of Gisborne. The money that I paid out to marksmen and Sheriff's men was never returned. I had to borrow more from a rich bishop nearby to continue my search, but the bishop now demands his money when he knows I have nothing with which to repay him. He will take my land and my castle and put myself and my daughter out."

"What is the sum you owe him?" asked Robin. "Please tell me."

"Four hundred gold pieces," said the knight.

Tears fell out of his eyes, and he turned to go away.

"Where are your friends?" asked Robin Hood.

"Robin," said Sir Richard, "they do not know me any more, for shame of my poverty."

"Come here," said Robin Hood to Little John, "and go to my treasure room, and bring me four hundred gold pieces. We are going to help a sad knight who has fallen into poverty."

Sir Richard blessed Robin, and thanked him countless times. Robin felt glad to help such a knight.

On that very evening Little John accompanied the knight on his way to the bishop's palace. The bishop was waiting there to take possession of the castle nearby unless Sir Richard paid him in full by sunset the next day.

When morning came, Sir Richard's daughter Marian was in the castle gathering up their few remaining goods, for she believed that they were losing the castle and land that day.

The bishop was sitting at his dinner table at home, when knocks on the door announced the knight was at the gate.

"Welcome, Sir Richard," said the porter. "The bishop and his men are waiting for you now."

The knight went forth and into the bishop's

hall, and kneeled down and saluted the bishop and his men, including Robin's enemy, the Sheriff of Nottingham. "I have come on the day of payment," said Sir Richard.

"Have you brought me my money?" said the bishop.

"Not one penny," said the knight.

"You are terribly in my debt," said the bishop, laughing. "Why are you here if you do not mean to pay me for the loan?"

"I ask you," said Sir Richard, "to give me more time."

"Your time is up," said the Sheriff, the bishop's friend.

"Please, good Sheriff," said Sir Richard, "won't you speak for me?"

"I will not do that," said the Sheriff.

"Then, good bishop," said Sir Richard, "allow me to be your servant till I may pay you back in full."

"No," said the bishop. "I have a fancy for your land."

"Do you not know," asked Sir Richard, "that it is good to help a friend in need?"

"Get out, poor man!" cried the bishop. "Get out of my hall!"

Sir Richard now jumped up and strode toward the bishop. At the bishop's feet he dropped a heavy sack. "Here is your gold, bishop," said the knight. "It is all the money that you loaned to me. Had you been decent to me I would have paid you more!"

The bishop sat still at his table, and could not eat another bite. Sir Richard turned and left the bishop's hall and rode home in triumph on his horse.

"Welcome, father," sweet Marian greeted him. "Is it true, then, that all we have is lost?"

"Be happy, my daughter," said Sir Richard. "And let us thank Robin Hood. He gave me gold to pay the bishop. If not for Robin's kindness, we would be beggars now."

Sir Richard then managed his land and estate so well that within one year he was able to return to Sherwood Forest and repay Robin all of his gold. In addition, as a present, he gave Robin a splendid feast and one hundred beautiful silver arrows, which very much pleased Robin's merry men. So began Robin's friendship with Sir Richard, and so began the fondness that Marian, the knight's daughter, felt for Robin.

Friar Tuck

IN SUMMERTIME, when the leaves grow green, and the flowers are fresh and bright, Robin Hood and his men were disposed to play. Some would leap, some would run, and some would shoot their bows. Will Stutely shot a target from three hundred feet, and Midge shot one from four hundred, and finally Little John shot one from five hundred.

"That's such a good shot," remarked Robin Hood, "I'd ride my horse a hundred miles to find an archer as fine as you, Little John."

This made Will Stutely laugh. "There lives a Friar Tuck who will beat both him and you. He can draw a bow so well, he'll beat all of us in a row." Will said the friar lived beyond Sherwood Forest by a stream, and he described the enormous and powerful friar so that anyone might know him.

Robin vowed then he wouldn't eat or drink till he saw this Friar Tuck. He put on his gear and his sword, and took his bow in hand. Wearing a sheaf of arrows at his belt, he set out on his horse.

When he passed through Sherwood Forest and came to the wide, cold stream he saw a strong, big man, whose head was round and shaved on top, though his face was bearded. He wore a loose brown robe and a string of prayer beads—these signs showed he was a friar. At his side he had a broadsword and a small shield.

Robin Hood saw that he had found his man and leapt off his horse. Then he approached the friar and said, "Carry me over this stream, Friar Tuck, or else your life is done."

The friar said nothing but set Robin Hood on his back and strode out into the water. When he got to the middle of the stream, without saying a word, he tossed Robin off his back into the water. "It's your choice," now said the friar, "whether you will sink or swim."

Robin Hood swam to the bank of the stream and so did Friar Tuck.

But Robin was angry and took his bow in hand and let fly an arrow at the friar. Friar Tuck blocked that arrow with the shield at his belt. Robin Hood shot till his arrows were gone. Then he and the friar took their swords and shields and fought like fierce beasts from ten o'clock that day till four in the afternoon.

Without saying a word, he tossed Robin off his
back into the water.

Finally Robin sank to his knees with weariness and asked the friar for a favor. "O Friar Tuck, I beg for a favor on my knees. Allow me to set my horn to my mouth and to blow a blast three times."

"That I will allow," said the friar. "I hope, indeed, you'll blow so hard your eyes and cheeks pop out."

Robin Hood set his horn to his mouth and blew loud three times. Fifty of his merry men with bows in hand came running from the forest. "Whose men are these," asked Friar Tuck, "that come so fast?"

"They are mine," said Robin. "What is it to you?"

"A favor, a favor," said the friar. "Grant me one, just as I granted one to you. Let me put my fingers to my mouth to whistle three times."

"I will let you," said Robin, "or else I should seem unfair."

The friar put two fingers to his mouth and whistled loudly three times. And just as soon as he did, fifty-two savage dogs came running to the friar. "For every man there's a dog," said Friar Tuck. "And for you, I myself and two!" The dogs at once went for Robin and tore off his cloak. Robin was bitten and nipped so hard he yelped.

Little John, seeing his master's danger, cried out to the friar, "Call off your dogs, or else I'll shoot them down."

"Hold your bow, friend," said Friar Tuck, for he loved his dogs quite well. "Do not shoot my pets, and your master and I will make a deal."

So Robin said, "Friar, if you will forsake this life by the stream, you may come and live with us in Sherwood, be our chaplain, and share our merriness, wine and gold."

Now Friar Tuck had lived here by the stream for more than seven years, and no one had been able to persuade him to leave . . . until Robin did this day. "I like your service, I think I'll join."

"Welcome, friend. My name is Robin Hood."

"And I am, as you know, good Friar Tuck."

Robin Hood and Allen a Dale

ROBIN HOOD was an outlaw, but he did poor men many good deeds. One day as Robin Hood stood under the leaves of the greenwood tree, he saw a young man come drooping along the way. Every step the young man took he sighed, "Oh, what a woeful day!"

Out from the trees at him stepped Little John and Midge the miller's son. The young man saw them, bent his bow and said, "Stand back! What do you want with me?"

"You need to come see our master under yonder greenwood tree," said Midge.

The young man nodded at the well-armed men and went along, and Robin asked, "Have you money to spare my men and me?"

"I have no money," the young man said, "except five pennies and a ring, a ring I've held for seven long years, to have it at my wedding. But yesterday, I was supposed to marry a maid, and she was taken from me and chosen to be, instead, an old knight's delight today."

"What is your name?" asked Robin Hood.

"My name is Allen a Dale."

"What will you give me, young Allen a Dale, to get you to your true love and your true love to you?"

"I have no money," the young man said, "but I would become one of your merry men if you could make that happen."

"How many miles is it to your true love, Allen?"

"It is only five miles."

Then Robin and his men and Allen set out across the plain. When Robin came to the church where Allen was to have been married, he left the men behind and entered.

"Why are you here?" the bishop asked Robin. The bishop was fat and rich and was there to perform the wedding ceremony.

"I am a good harper," said Robin Hood, "the best in the north of England."

"O welcome, o welcome," the bishop then said, clasping Robin by the hand. "Harp music delights me."

"But you shall have no music," said Robin Hood, pulling away. He did not like fat bishops. "You shall have no music till I see the bride and groom."

And just then in came a wealthy knight, Sir Twaddle, who was solemn, gray and old, and after him came a splendidly dressed young lady, Suzanne Marie, who was as beautiful and bright as gold.

"This is not a fitting match," said Robin Hood.

"How dare you," said Sir Twaddle. "Who are you to say such a thing?"

"The bride's protector," said Robin, "that's who."

"I have her consent," said the knight.

"Consent is not desire," said Robin. "I declare that the bride shall choose her own dear one."

"Thank you, good man," said Suzanne Marie, well pleased.

Then Robin Hood put his horn to his mouth and blew two or three blasts. Twenty-four of his archers leaped over the churchyard walls and came marching into the church. The first to come in was Allen a Dale.

"He is my dear one," cried the beautiful bride, "Allen a Dale."

"She is my dear one," said Allen a Dale, "Suzanne Marie."

"You each have found your true love," said Robin to Allen. "And you shall be married today."

"That shall not be," said the bishop, "for you have no right. Your blessing will not count."

"No right? Why not?"

"Because I am the bishop, I am a man of the cloth! This coat gives me my right."

Robin Hood clutched the bishop's arm, said, "Excuse me, please," and pulled off the bishop's coat and handed it to Friar Tuck. He was as large as the bishop was fat, and was able to pull it on. "I declare," said Robin, "this coat makes you the right man, Friar Tuck."

"Then I may marry the true loves?" asked Friar Tuck.

"Does the coat give him the right?" Robin Hood asked the bishop.

Now the bishop was not a brave man, and the men's swords and bows scared him quite a lot. He agreed and said, "Yes, he has the right, beggarly friar though he be."

"And you, Sir Twaddle, do you agree that Suzanne Marie should marry the man she loves, a man as fresh as spring, and not a man in the depth of winter?"

Sir Twaddle was a good man, but an old man, and he could not help but see that Suzanne Marie and Allen a Dale were as matched as matched could be. "I resign my claim," he said sadly. "I admit defeat. I see where love is and where it is not. I bless both him and Suzanne Marie."

"You are very gracious," said Robin.

"I am very sad," said Sir Twaddle. "If you don't mind," he said now, his head low, "I will take myself away before the wedding begins."

"I, too, will go my way," said the bishop.

"Sir Twaddle, please take your leave," said Robin, "and we are sorry for your sorrow. But as for you, dear bishop, we like your company. We shall be glad of your seal and signature when the wedding is over. Please stay."

And now Robin bent his bow at the bishop and asked if the bishop would like to hear the twang of his harp.

"No, not at all," said the bishop. "That is not the harp music I enjoy."

When humble Friar Tuck in a bishop's coat went to take his position, the people began to laugh. "Who gives this maid to be married?" asked Friar Tuck.

"I do!" said Robin Hood. The bride looked like a queen.

"And who gives this man?"

No one answered, so Robin nudged the bishop, who stuttered and then sang, "I do!"

Allen a Dale returned with his wife to Sherwood Forest, where the merry men built them a little house beside the lodge. Allen a Dale enjoyed his life as an outlaw, and Suzanne Marie enjoyed her life as the wife of the happiest outlaw in Robin's troop. The men envied Allen's happiness, and Robin did too. "I think we merry men need wives," said Robin. "Or we all shall be miserable."

Guy of Gisborne

ONE MORNING in springtime Robin Hood had a dream. He woke and told it to his men.

"I thought two men, one who seemed a wild beast, the other someone I know, beat and bound me and took my bow from me." Robin thought a moment and said, "If my name is Robin Hood, I'll take revenge on those two."

"Indeed that's your name, good master," said Little John. "But don't be hasty to read your dream. Dreams are strange and as unpredictable as the wind, which blows quickly over a hill tonight and yet tomorrow may be still."

But Robin Hood would not heed such talk. "I'm going to seek these men of my dream in the forest. Little John will go with me." They covered themselves in their green cloaks and went till they came within sight of the greenwood tree. There they saw a hulking man, clothed in horsehide from head to toe, who was leaning against the tree. The sword and dagger at the man's side had been the death of many men. It was from his dream that Robin recognized this loathsome man!

"Stay here," said Little John to Robin, "behind this grove, and I will go to this man and find out what he wants."

"How often have I sent my men ahead and stayed behind, John? Why shouldn't I go myself to this man and discover his business?" Now Robin, in bad spirits from his disturbing dream, was cruel to his friend and said, "If I thought my bow wouldn't break, John, I'd hit it over your head."

These words so angered Little John, that he scowled and stalked away. He sulkily wandered till he heard a shout, and near the town he found his fellows chasing after the Sheriff's men, who had just shot two of Robin's. Little John swore to himself, "I'll shoot that Sheriff, and please my friends and master."

Little John went after the Sheriff on his own, and discovered him safe in Nottingham's town square. Little John, undisguised and unhidden, bent his bow at the Sheriff and made to shoot, but the bow was made of poor wood and snapped in two. This attracted the attention of the Sheriff's men. "Woe to you, wicked wood," said Little John. "Today you have vexed me when I needed your help."

The Sheriff's men rushed at Little John and captured him and tied him to a post.

"You shall be chopped up and down till you are dead and then hanged upon a tree," said the Sheriff to Little John. The Sheriff hated Robin and Robin's men more than any man should hate.

Let us leave talking of Little John, for he is tied up for now, and speak instead of the fearsome Guy of Gisborne and Robin Hood, under the greenwood tree.

"Good morning, good man," said Sir Guy of Gisborne.

"Good morning, good sir," said Robin Hood. "By the look of your bow, I think you must be a good archer."

Guy of Gisborne nodded and said, "I am fair enough. But I'm unsure of my way."

"Then I'll guide you through the forest, friend," said Robin Hood.

"I'm looking for an outlaw," said Sir Guy. "Men call him Robin Hood. I'd rather meet him than find a pile of gold."

"It might be better for you if you don't," said Robin. "Let's have a contest, meanwhile, friend. We'll walk in the woods and shoot at marks."

Robin wanted to test his foe and so led the fierce man along.

"That bump on the log," said Robin, pointing his arm. "Whoever comes closest, will win the first round." Guy of Gisborne was an expert archer, but he could not at first see the mark.

"What log?" said Sir Guy.

"Through those trees, and beyond that meadow, there lies a log."

"Ah," said Sir Guy, narrowing his eyes. "Ah, I think I see. But what bump?"

"On the left, down along the side. There it is," said Robin, pointing again, "about the size of a nut."

"Hmm," said Guy of Gisborne. "I cannot see it."

"There!" said Robin. He plucked his bow and sent off an arrow. In a moment, Sir Guy could see the log and the arrow, like a flag, waving from it. "There is the bump," said Robin.

Sir Guy was surprised at the wonderful shot, and he strung his bow and himself let an arrow fly. Sir Guy hit the log, but they discovered, when they had walked out from the trees and over the meadow, that it was Robin's arrow only that struck the bump.

"You shoot very well," said Sir Guy.

"No," said Robin, "not I. I'm just fair enough."

"Let me choose the target this time," said Sir Guy.

"Please do," said Robin.

"I choose," said Guy of Gisborne, thinking evil thoughts, "I choose the cap upon your head. That will be our mark."

"Very well," said Robin. "Who shall shoot first?"

"I shall," said Sir Guy. "Please stand by that tree."

Robin strode over to the tree, and stood his ground. He lifted his chin, tapped his cap down tight on his head, folded his arms across his chest, and called out, "Shoot away!"

Guy of Gisborne thought this man was quite silly. He was tempted to shoot the man and not the cap. He notched his arrow, he squinted at Robin, he pulled the string, and the arrow shot out. At the last moment Robin ducked and then shouted, "Good shot, my friend, good shot!" For Robin's cap was stuck dead to the tree.

"Now," said Robin, "it's my turn. I don't think I can top that."

Sir Guy turned pink. He was very angry with this clown. He had tried to kill Robin with that shot, and now he had to allow Robin to shoot at him!

Robin handed Sir Guy his torn cap, and Sir Guy, patting it up, put it gently on his head.

"Now hold still," called out Robin. "No moving." Robin made ready, but then held his string. "Good, sir," he called. "Sir? If I shoot the cap from further away, does that mean I win?"

"No," called back Sir Guy. "We shall shoot till someone misses." Sir Guy planned to miss his next shot and strike his foe in the heart.

"Here she flies!" cried Robin. Sir Guy was brave yet he could not help but close his eyes. Robin plucked his bow and away flew the arrow.

Sir Guy waited and waited and then waited some more, his eyes still closed. He was waiting for the sound of the arrow to pass by. "Shoot!" he cried out. "Shoot the arrow, young man!"

"I shot it," said Robin quietly. "Now open your eyes."

Sir Guy opened his eyes and then felt for the cap upon his head. It was there, the cap was still on his head! "Ha, ha, young fellow, you have missed your mark!"

As Sir Guy gleefully held out Robin's cap to return it, out of the blue sky, high from above the greenwood tree, dropped an arrow, straight down through the cap! Sir Guy was so startled, his eyes bulged out.

"Who are you?" he cried. "What a shot! Tell me your name, friend." Now Guy of Gisborne was the most terrible man ever to set foot in Sherwood Forest, and yet this fool had amazed him. "Tell me."

"No, no," said Robin, "not till you've first told me yours, my friend."

"I come from far away, over the hills and dales. I've done many wicked deeds, I must admit. Today I murder Robin Hood for a bounty from the Sheriff. The Sheriff, indeed, is rounding up that outlaw's men right now, to rid him of all pests. My name," he said bowing, "is Guy of Gisborne."

"My name," bowed Robin, "is Robin Hood, the man you seek."

It was a splendid sight then, to see how these two men went at each other with their shining swords for two hours that summer day. Neither man could hit the other, but their swords sang out like angry steel.

"You are a dead man!" cried Sir Guy.

"Not before you will be," said Robin.

Both warriors began to stagger, their swords screeched up and down. Robin seemed the weaker at first, but then it seemed Sir Guy. Finally they had battled so that their swords were crossed, and Sir Guy gave Robin Hood a shove, and Robin went tumbling down.

"Oh," cried Robin, "it can't have been my

fate to die today." With these words, and with Guy about to strike him dead, Robin leaped up again and found a target on his foe. He swung his sword and killed the fearsome Guy.

Weary Robin stood over his foe. "Lie there, wicked Guy of Gisborne, and don't be angry with me if you've received worse wounds than I. You will now receive better clothes." And so Robin switched his clothes with Sir Guy, and clad himself head to toe in his foe's leather, bloody though it was. "I need a new disguise," said Robin Hood, "to repay that Sheriff who offered you a prize."

Robin took up Sir Guy's bow and arrows and horn, and went off to Nottingham, where Little John was tied to a post awaiting death. When Robin entered the town he blew Sir Guy's horn and sent a blast the Sheriff heard.

"Listen," said the Sheriff, "I hear good news. Sir Guy's horn has blown, and he has killed Robin Hood."

At this Little John groaned.

"Here comes Sir Guy in his suit of horse-hide," said the Sheriff. "Greetings, my fear-some Sir Guy of Gisborne. Ask for your reward and you'll receive it."

"I don't want gold," said Robin Hood. "And I

don't want land. Now that I have slain the master, let me strike down his second in command. That's all I ask."

"You're a madman," said the Sheriff. "You could have had riches. But since you've so asked, so will you receive."

Now Little John had heard his master speak and knew well it was his voice. The disguise could not hide his true friend Robin from him, and he knew he would soon be freed.

As Robin Hood went towards Little John, the Sheriff and his men followed to watch Little John's death.

"Get back," cried Robin Hood. "Why are you crowding me? It's not the custom where I come from for others to hear a man's last words."

The Sheriff and his men retreated, and Robin pulled out a knife and cut loose Little John. He gave Little John Sir Guy's bow and arrows and told him to flee. But John took Sir Guy's bow and bloody arrows and took an aim at the Sheriff. The Sheriff turned to run away and so did the Sheriff's men. The Sheriff received an arrow high up on his thigh, and tumbled to the ground. His men had to pull him up and take him home, and Little John felt avenged.

Robin pulled out a knife and cut loose Little John.

"Friends again?" asked Little John, offering Robin his hand.

Robin Hood said, laughing, "Of course, my fellow. The blame was all on me." Forever after Robin remembered his insult to Little John, and greatly regretted his temper.

Robin Hood and Little
John Meet Their Kin

IN NOTTINGHAM there lived a tanner, a man who turned hides into leather. His name was Arthur a Bland, and he was as tough as the leather he made. One summer morning he went into Sherwood Forest to see the King's deer that range among the trees, and there he met Robin Hood.

"Hold on there, young fellow," said Robin Hood, bending his bow at the tanner. "What is your business here? You look to me like a thief, one who comes to shoot at the King's deer. I must ask you to halt."

"I think I will not," said the tanner. "But if you try to stop me I shall put a knot on your head with my long oak staff."

At this Robin Hood unbuckled his belt and laid down his longbow and arrows. He took up his own staff of oak that was both stiff and strong. "I shall use your weapon," said Robin, "since you will not back down from mine."

"My staff is made of oak, and it will knock down a bull, and I think it will also knock down you. So take care," said Arthur a Bland.

Robin Hood was angry at these words and swung his long oak staff. He clipped the tanner on the head so hard that Arthur wandered in a short circle before he could shake himself back awake. He brushed the blood from off his face and took a swing at Robin.

The tanner's club found its mark, and toppled Robin Hood to the ground. The blood now dyed Robin Hood's dark hair red, but before Arthur could deliver another blow, up leapt Robin, and about and about they went, darting and lunging, like two wild beasts.

Finally, Robin Hood said, "Hold your hand, hold your hand, and let us end our quarrel. From now on, you are free to roam the woods of Sherwood."

"I have my staff to thank for that gift, not you," said Arthur, still rather angry.

"Come, come," said Robin Hood, "tell me what you do for a living. And where do you live?"

"I am a tanner," Arthur answered, "and I have worked for a long time in Nottingham. I give you my promise that if you come into town, I will tan your hide for free."

Robin laughed. "Well, good friend, since you are willing to be so kind to me, I will return the favor. But if you give up this tanning trade, and live in the green forest with me and my men, I swear by my name, which is Robin

Hood, that I will pay you gold and dress you in our Lincoln green."

"If you are Robin Hood," said Arthur a Bland, "then I will never leave. Because, please tell me, where is Little John? He is the one of whom I want to hear. For his mother is my aunt, and my mother is his aunt, and we are cousins."

Robin Hood blew on his bugle horn loudly and quite shrilly, and Little John quickly appeared running down a grassy hill. "What has happened?" cried out Little John. "Master, tell me what is the matter?"

"It's this tanner," said Robin Hood. "He is a strong young man and master of his business. He has tanned my hide quite well."

"He is to be praised," said Little John, "if he really did do that. But if he is that strong, then he and I shall have a fight, and he can try to tan my hide as well." Little John pounded his staff upon the ground and nodded at the man.

"No, dear Little John," said Robin Hood, "I understand that this man is a relative of yours. His name is Arthur a Bland."

Then Little John tossed the staff as far away as he could fling it, and threw himself upon Arthur a Bland and hung around his neck. Little John and Arthur wept for joy. Then Robin Hood smiled and called them back to join him under the greenwood tree to celebrate.

The summer went on, and the forest had not yielded many people for Robin Hood and his men to rob. The deer were scarce, as they had been killed by many besides Robin and his men. "We have no vittles," announced Robin. So he and the men set out separately to see what they each could find.

It was in the middle of the day when Robin met the fanciest man that had ever walked through the forest. The man's shirt was made of silk, and his stockings were scarlet red. As he walked on along his way, he did not notice Robin, but instead spied a fine herd of deer.

"Now the best of all you deer," declared the stranger, "I shall have for my dinner."

The stranger took no time at all to pull out his bow and bend it deep. And in an instant he shot, from a long distance, the best of the herd.

"Good shot! Good shot!" called out Robin Hood then. "That shot was as good as a man can make, and if you will accept, you shall become one of my merry men."

"Rather than that, why don't you go cut up and prepare my deer? Get to it now, or with my fist I'll make you sore," said the stranger.

"You had better not try that," said Robin

Hood, "because though I seem an easy mark, all alone, if I just blow my horn I can have several dozen men who will join my side."

"No matter how fast you blow your horn," the stranger said, "I can pluck my bow just as fast and stop your breath."

Robin Hood was angry and pulled out his bow to shoot, and the stranger just as quickly bent his bow at Robin. They stood poised, ready to shoot, each waiting for the other to flinch. "Hold on, hold on!" said Robin Hood, lowering his bow. "We are at a standstill. Let's instead take our swords and shields and fight our fight under that tree."

"Fair enough," said the stranger. "I will not flee."

They swung their swords and gave each other a powerful blow across the shield. They both almost fell over faint. "Let's take a rest," said Robin. And then he and the stranger sat down under the greenwood tree.

"Oh, my goodness," said Robin. "You are a mighty man, aren't you? Tell me who you are, and tell me why you have come."

"I shall tell you," said the stranger. "I was born and bred in Maxfield, and my name is Young Gamwell. I am looking for an uncle of mine, some call him Robin Hood."

"You are a relative of Robin Hood's? We should not have fought at all."

"I am his sister's son."

"Then I am your mother's brother!" said Robin Hood. And he and Young Gamwell leapt to their feet and hugged and cried.

Little John now came along this trail near the tree and said, "Oh, master, where have you been all day?"

"I met this stranger," said Robin Hood, all bloody. "He has given me a terrible drubbing."

"Then I shall have a fight with him," said Little John, "and see if he can beat me."

"Oh no, oh no," said Robin Hood. "Little John, that may not be. For he is my own sister's son, my nephew who is dear to me. He shall become one of our merry men, and Scarlet shall we call him. We will be the bravest outlaws in all of England."

"Very well," said Little John. "Now who shot that deer over there? For the men are hungry."

"My nephew did the deed," said Robin Hood. "Let us shoot several more and make a feast."

"Very good, dear master," said Little John. And Little John and Robin Hood and Scarlet plucked their bows and killed deer for their feast.

The Monk and the
Capture of Robin Hood

"THIS IS a merry morning," said Little John. "And a merrier man than I does not live. Pluck up your heart, dear master, and see that it's a beautiful morning in May."

"No, there is something that grieves my heart," said Robin Hood. "It makes my heart ache. I haven't been to church for two weeks. Today I will go to Nottingham."

"Then take twelve of your men, well armed, master, so no one dare try to kill you," said Midge.

"No," said Robin, "I will take no men but Little John, who shall bear my bow till I need it."

"You shall bear yours and I shall bear mine, and along our way we shall shoot at marks for pennies," said Little John. They shot at targets until Little John had won five pennies from his master. Now Robin Hood was the best of shots, but this morning shot much worse than usual.

Little John was proud and laughed at his

luck, and started thinking of ways to spend his pennies in town. But Robin Hood grew riled and called Little John a cheat, and slapped his friend's broad face.

"If you were not my master," cried Little John, "I'd clobber you or run you through. Get yourself a new man, for you have lost me now."

So Robin Hood went alone to Nottingham that morning, and Little John made his way back to his friends.

When Robin walked into Nottingham, he prayed that he would get out safe again. In St. Mary's Church he listened to a sermon. Everyone at church looked at him, and wondered that he was there. Down along the aisle strode a huge monk, who knew Robin Hood as soon as he saw him. He stopped at Robin's pew and gaped for one moment, before continuing past. The monk, who once was robbed by Robin, hoped to take revenge. He sneaked out now and had all the gates of Nottingham locked, and then went and found the Sheriff, who was fast asleep. "Get up, hurry, get ready!" cried the monk. "I have spotted the outlaw Robin Hood, he is in at the Mass. It's your fault, lazy Sheriff, if he gets away."

The Sheriff got up and quickly got ready, and gathered around himself many men. They came to the church and burst through the doors. Robin turned and saw the men, and said to himself, "Alas! Now I miss the company of my friend Little John."

As the Sheriff's men approached, Robin gave up, rather than fight in church. The Sheriff was gleeful. Crowing over the man he had long sought, he said, "Try to escape me this time, you outlaw!"

Indeed, Robin now doubted that he should be able to escape, and did not answer the Sheriff. Robin remembered how he himself had been cruel to Little John and, without Little John's help, Robin thought he was sure to die on the gallows or in prison.

The Sheriff set sorry Robin into the farthest, deepest cell in the jail. The Sheriff then sent off the happy monk on a trip to the King with a letter about the capture, requesting the King's wishes as to the fate of the famous bandit.

When Robin Hood did not return that day to the greenwood tree in Sherwood Forest, his men grew uneasy, especially Little John. He had not forgiven Robin Hood the slap on the cheek, but he also had not forgiven himself for allowing his friend to enter Nottingham alone. He and Midge stopped a passing carter on the road from town and asked for any news. "News?" said the carter. "Yes, the Sheriff has captured the good man Robin Hood. The monk, the one who hated Robin Hood, has set out for the King in London to tell him of the news. The Sheriff and monk expect rewards—"

"And I will be sure to give one to them," said Little John, thinking of revenge. "Thank you, carter."

Midge and Little John set out to block the monk's path. They stole two horses and made great haste, and caught up to the monk the next morning. They greeted him as if they were his friends, and asked him from where he had journeyed.

"I come from Nottingham," said the monk. He did not trust these men and wondered who they were. "And from where might you two come?" he asked.

"We come from the south, and yet we heard some news that cheered our hearts," said Midge, for Little John was too angry with the monk to speak. "We want to hear about that outlaw Robin Hood who was captured yesterday. He robbed me and my friend last year of a sack of gold. If that outlaw has been taken, we'll be quite content."

"So did he rob me of more than that," said the monk. He now trusted these men of

Robin's. "I was the one who caused his arrest. You may thank me for it."

"Yes," said Little John, his voice a growl, "indeed we soon will."

Midge spoke up, "We would like to go with you on your way. You know that outlaw Robin Hood has many wild men, and if you ride this way alone, you'll almost certainly be killed."

"Oh!" said the monk.

Before they went very much further, Midge took the bridle of the monk's horse, and Little John took the monk by the cowl and pulled him off the horse. The monk cried out for mercy.

"Mercy?" said Little John. "That was my master that you brought to harm. You'll never get to our King to tell him your tale."

"No, indeed," said Midge. "You'll be spending the rest of your life among Robin's men, unless indeed Robin returns to us." They took the Sheriff's letter to the King that the monk had kept under his shirt, and then Midge tied the monk's horse to his and led him back to Sherwood Forest while Little John, as the monk's substitute, went on to London.

When Little John arrived at the King's court, he fell on his knees. "God save the King," he said, and handed over the Sheriff's letter.

The King, reading the letter, cried out, "Hurrah!" When he finished, however, he was puzzled and asked, "But where is the monk who was supposed to bring this news?"

"He was too frightened of Robin Hood's men to pass through the forest, and so he asked me if I would take his place," said Little John. "I myself am not afraid of those merry outlaw men."

The King said Little John was a brave man, made him a present of a bag of gold, and named him a Royal Officer. His highness bid him return to Nottingham and tell the Sheriff to bring Robin Hood, unharmed, to him.

Little John, outfitted as a Royal Officer, now took the road back to Nottingham. When he arrived, however, the gates were barred, and Little John called out to the gatekeeper, "Why are the gates barred?"

"Because of Robin Hood," said the gatekeeper. "He's been tossed in our prison and Robin Hood's men have been trying to break in to free him."

"They haven't been able to rescue him, then?" said Little John.

"No, not even close," said the gatekeeper. "And are you the Royal Officer who has come as his escort?"

"That I am. I shall escort him out of Nottingham as soon as I can."

Little John went through the town then and found the Sheriff to give him the King's orders.

"And what happened to the good monk I sent to the King?" asked the Sheriff. He did not recognize this hulking man as Little John, the man he had once hired, the man he had once tied to a post and was about to hang.

"The King is so fond of the monk," lied Little John, "that he has made him the abbot of Westminster."

The Sheriff was delighted with the news of such a reward. If the monk had earned such a prize, what would the Sheriff's be? The Sheriff was too excited to suspect Little John any longer. He gave him a grand dinner and served him the finest wine. That night, after the Sheriff went to bed, Little John slipped through the town to the prison, called out to the jailer and asked him to get up.

"Get up?" cried the jailer. "Why should I?"

"Because," said Little John, "I am a Royal Officer, and your prisoner Robin Hood has escaped."

The jailer ran out to Little John and begged for pardon. "Please help me," said the jailer.

"Perhaps you may help me," said Little John.

"If ever I may, I will," said the jailer.

"Let us go see the cell from which he escaped," said Little John.

"Yes," said the jailer. "Let us see."

When they arrived at the cell, the jailer took his keys and opened the door. The dark, heavy door creaked. The cell was pitch black. But the jailer was surprised that when he held up a torch, there was Robin Hood fast asleep, sharing with a mouse a bed of straw.

"Why," whispered the jailer, with surprise and relief, "this is Robin Hood indeed."

"Go see," said Little John. "Go wake him and see."

As the jailer trembled, Robin Hood sat up and saw his dear Little John at the door.

"Little John!" said he.

"Hello, Robin," said Little John.

"It is he! Robin Hood!" said the jailer, jumping back.

"So I am!" said Robin Hood. "But for the rest of the night, you shall take my place."

Little John laughed with joy and said, "Thank you, jailer, for your help. We mean no harm to you, so if you stay here quietly, we shall let you live."

"I shall be quiet," said the jailer, "as quiet as this mouse." And he sat down on the straw where Robin Hood had been and watched Little John and Robin Hood close the door.

There was Robin Hood fast asleep, sharing with a
mouse a bed of straw.

When the Sheriff came that morning with his men to take Robin Hood away to the King, he found instead the jailer and a mouse asleep inside. "Where is Robin Hood?" cried the Sheriff.

"The King's deputy has already taken him, sir," said the jailer.

"But when? And why are you here?"

"This morning, sir, before the cock did crow. I admit I did not know, sir, that the King had made one of Robin Hood's men, Little John, the messenger for his fate."

"Little John!" said the Sheriff. He and his men ran out to the town gates, and the gate-keeper gave them the news that Robin Hood had been safely escorted out several hours before.

Already, Robin Hood and his men were celebrating under the greenwood tree deep in Sherwood Forest. Robin had apologized to Little John for his slap on the cheek and had offered to be Little John's own servant, but that was something Little John would not allow.

The men were glad to have Robin Hood back safe and sound. They released the monk, who felt lucky to still have his life, and he returned to Nottingham. "If I ever see Robin

Hood in church again," said he, "then I will walk by and say nothing but 'Bless him!' "

The Sheriff could get no one to go after Robin Hood in the forest, and he had no one to send to the King. And so he went to London himself with the distressing news that Robin Hood, the kingdom's most famous outlaw, had escaped again. He expected the King would have his head, and sad as could be was he.

But the King had mercy on the Sheriff. "This Little John, Sheriff, has tricked you, but he also tricked me. And so I pardon you, I pardon me, and I now also pardon Little John and Robin Hood, for there are no such heroes in all England. Little John was true to his master and fooled us all!"

Robin Hood and the Tinker

ONE DAY, as Robin Hood was walking towards Nottingham, he met a tinker, a man who fixed pots and pans. The tinker was a large, strong man, and Robin Hood politely said hello and asked, "Have you any news? You go from town to town, tell me what you have heard."

"All the news I have is my own," said the tinker. "I have a warrant from the King to arrest the daring outlaw Robin Hood wherever I find him. If you can tell me where he is, I will give you a small reward. The King will give me a hundred gold coins if I can bring that man before him, so if we can now arrest him, we shall be as rich as rich can be."

"Let me see that warrant, friend," said Robin Hood. "If it looks right, I will do the best I can so that we might catch him tonight."

"I will not show you," said the tinker. "I will not trust anyone with it. If you will not tell me where he is, I must go and try to trap him on my own."

51

"If you will go to Nottingham with me," said Robin, "I know we shall find him."

The tinker squinted at Robin Hood and Robin squinted at the tinker. "May I trust you?" asked the tinker.

"As well as I may trust you," said Robin.

The tinker had a long, knotty staff and Robin had a good long knife, and, looking each other over again, they nodded and set out for Nottingham. In the town they came to an inn where they might spend the night and drink. They both called for beer and wine. But the tinker drank so fast he lost his wits and fell asleep.

Robin Hood searched the tinker's coat till he found the warrant and the tinker's money-bag. "I shall keep both of these for you," said Robin to his dozing friend.

"Who is paying the bill for the beer and wine?" the innkeeper asked Robin.

"My friend will pay the bill," said Robin. "He also needs a room in which to sleep. Good-night."

When the tinker woke up in the morning and saw that his companion was gone, he called for the innkeeper. "I had a king's warrant for the arrest of the daring outlaw Robin Hood, and now it is gone. I had a bag of money, and now that is gone. I cannot pay you. The man who promised to be my friend has run away and robbed me."

"That friend you mention," said the innkeeper, "they call him Robin Hood. When you met him, you should have known he would do you no good."

"Had I known it was he, I would have arrested him and had my reward. In the meantime, innkeeper, I must go away. I will go and find him, whatever happens to me. Now, how much do I owe you?"

"Ten pennies," said the innkeeper.

"I will pay very soon," said the tinker, "or else you may keep my workbag, and my good tinkering hammer too."

"The only way you might find him and catch him," said the innkeeper, "is while he's out alone in the forest shooting the King's deer."

The tinker ran off into the forest until he found Robin Hood hunting deer. The tinker did not hide himself at all, but strode directly at his foe.

"Who is this fool," said Robin Hood, "that is coming toward me here?"

"No fool, no fool," said the tinker. "If you want to know who has done whom most wrong, just watch my crab-tree staff."

Robin drew his sharp steel sword, but the tinker got his blows in fast and bruised Robin black and blue.

"One moment, one moment!" cried out Robin Hood. "Grant me, please, one moment."

"Before I grant you a moment, I'll hang you from this tree," said the tinker. But when he turned to see if any of Robin's men were approaching, Robin blew his horn, and in three instants Little John and Will Stutely came.

"What is the matter again?" said Little John. Robin Hood often got himself into difficulties like these.

"This tinker here has hammered my body," said Robin.

"Let us see," said Little John, "what he can do with me."

"No," said Robin. "I wish to see this quarrel cease. I want us all to live in peace. Let us give the jolly tinker a reward, as much as the King offered in ransom for me. He is a mighty man, and I should prefer he be on our side than against us."

The tinker was quite content with this and made his peace with Robin. He took the bag of gold that Little John offered and returned to Nottingham to pay the innkeeper and claim his tools.

The Sheriff's Man

IT WAS a bright, sunny day, and the young men who lived in Nottingham town held a shooting contest. Little John was wandering through the forest seeking to shoot the King's deer when he overheard shouts and cheers. His face was newly shaven and he was sure no one would know him, so he made his way down to the town and went among the young men, asking if he might shoot with them. A contest was as irresistible to Little John as it was to Robin Hood.

Three times Little John shot and each time he slit the mark. The Sheriff of Nottingham, who also enjoyed contests, had come to watch and was standing by the target. He did not recognize Little John as one of Robin Hood's men, and exclaimed, "Astounding! This man is the best archer that I ever saw."

He said to Little John, "Tell me now, brave young man, what is your name? Where were you born, and where do you live?"

"In Yorkshire, sir, I was born," said Little John, "and men call me ... " (Little John was thinking up a false name) "Reynold Greenleaf."

"Tell me, Rey Greenleaf, won't you work for me? It's good service and good pay. As one of my men, you just might win the reward for capturing the outlaw Robin Hood."

Little John thought it would be a good joke on the Sheriff to let himself be hired, and he agreed. The Sheriff granted him a good horse and a servant, and Little John began to live in the quarters next to the Sheriff's house. Even with the luxuries of a town life, Little John soon missed Robin Hood and the fellows. He asked the Sheriff if he could return to his old master.

"And who is your old master?" asked the Sheriff.

"A ranger," said Little John. For it was true, Robin Hood ranged far and wide over Sherwood Forest.

"You may return to your ranger," said the Sheriff, "as soon as the year is up."

"A year? But I am unhappy, master. This life does not suit me. I prefer an outdoor life."

"You are mine for a year, wretch. Is the duty too hard, or are you too lazy? I thought highly of you, young man, and now I do not. Even so, you are not leaving my service."

"Then," grumbled Little John to himself,

"then I shall be the worst servant you have ever had."

The next day, the Sheriff went out hunting, and Little John, instead of accompanying him, as was his duty, swore he had a stomachache and stayed in bed. Thinking of the jolly old days under the greenwood tree, which were not so very far in the past, Little John became hungry. "Good steward," he called out to the man who served the Sheriff's men their meals. "I beg you, bring me my lunch."

After a few moments, the steward, a small, earnest, hard-working man, loyal to the Sheriff, came into Little John's room and shook his head at him. "No lunch for those who don't work," said the steward. "No lunch for those with bellyaches. So says the Sheriff, lazy Reynold Greenleaf."

"Bring me my lunch, steward," said Little John, "or I'll crack your head."

The steward, who was two feet shorter than Little John and wise with his years, quickly returned to the kitchen and locked the food cupboards. When Little John slowly rose from bed to come crack his head, he ran out of the house. Then Little John gave one of the cupboards such a kick, it opened like a door. Little John helped himself to a stock of food, ale and wine. He was eating like a bear when the cook, a stout, sturdy man, walked in. "Who crashed in my cupboard door, Rey Greenleaf?"

"That must have been I," calmly said Little John.

"Who told you you could help yourself to the Sheriff's food?" said the cook.

"I must have told myself," said Little John, not stopping in his feast but eating even more.

The cook walked over to Little John and smacked him on the head three times with a spoon. "Get out of my kitchen," said the cook.

"Oh," said Little John, "three times you smacked me, and three times will you be smacked. And then I will finish my meal."

After Little John had smacked the cook with a spoon three times in return, he meant to sit down, but the cook pulled out his sword, and so Little John did the same. They fought bitterly, but neither could harm the other, though they went on for an hour. "I vow," said Little John, "you're one of the best swordsmen that ever yet I saw. If you could shoot as well with a bow as you duel with a sword, you should come back with me to the forest, where I return today, to live again with Robin Hood and his merry fellows."

"Put away your sword," said the cook, "and friends we will be." Then he cooked up a bigger feast than five men usually eat, and he and Little John shared the best meat, bread and wine in the Sheriff's kitchen. Before they set out to join Robin Hood, they went to the Sheriff's treasure drawers and broke open the steel locks. They took away all the Sheriff's silverware, money and drinking cups and went off on the Sheriff's horses to Robin Hood in Sherwood Forest.

"How do you do, master?" said Little John.

"Welcome to you, Little John," said Robin Hood, "and welcome to the good man you have brought. Have you enjoyed your service with the Sheriff?"

"Of course not, master," said Little John. "It was a change of pace for two weeks, but when I asked to be allowed to return to my old life, he would not allow it. But look, today the Sheriff himself sends me back to you with his own cook, his own silverware, money, drinking cups and horses."

"He sent you and the cook and the goods willingly? I doubt this," said Robin Hood.

"He's happy to be rid of me, I assure you," said Little John.

Little John decided to go find the Sheriff in the forest and get his consent. He did not want Robin to doubt his word, which, as we know, was so far quite false. He ran off five miles along trails and through woods until he found the Sheriff hunting with hounds and horn. Little John rushed towards him and knelt down. "My dear master!" he exclaimed.

"Lazybones Reynold Greenleaf," said the Sheriff, "why are you here and not asleep with an aching belly as I left you?"

"I am better and have been in the forest, and I have seen a beautiful sight. Over there, not far, I saw a gorgeous deer, whose color is green! Green, indeed! And that deer has one hundred and forty in his herd with him. Their horns are so sharp, master, that I dared not shoot at them for fear they would have slashed me."

"I tell you," said the Sheriff, "I have got to see this."

"Come along, then, dear master, and I'll lead you."

The Sheriff rode, and Little John ran, and when they came to the greenwood tree, out leaped Robin Hood. Little John said, "Look, sir Sheriff, there's the leader of the deer!"

The Sheriff, a sorry man, sat still on his horse. "Curse you, Reynold Greenleaf, you have betrayed me!"

"I swear," said Little John, "it is your own fault, because you ordered the steward not to serve me my lunch. After all, you would not allow me to leave your service, and a man in service needs to eat."

"I wish that I had allowed you to leave, certainly," said the Sheriff.

"Then have I your consent to leave your service and to collect my pay?" asked Little John.

"I wish I had never seen you," said the Sheriff. "Of course you should leave my service. As for your pay, you hardly earned a penny."

"Too cheap," said Little John. "Too cheap."

Soon enough, as was the custom when Robin Hood detained any man, the Sheriff was seated at Robin Hood's table and served a supper. But when the Sheriff saw his own cups and silver on the table, he was so sad he could not eat. "Cheer up," said Robin Hood, "because, Sheriff, I shall spare your life."

When they had all eaten well, the day was gone, and Robin Hood told the Sheriff to put on the green cloak of the merry men. "As Little John was made to serve you, so shall you serve me. I shall teach you how to be an outlaw."

"Before I am here another night, Robin Hood, living such a life," said the Sheriff, "I pray to you to kill me. I would forgive you for doing so. Or better yet, be charitable, and let me go, and I shall be the best friend you and your men ever had."

"Swear me an oath, then," said Robin, "on my sword, that you shall never plot harm to me or to any of my men."

The Sheriff, lying in his heart, swore the oath and was allowed to go, though without his gold or silver, which, said Robin Hood, was a good trade for Little John's service.

The Golden Arrow

THE SHERIFF of Nottingham grieved and grieved about the trick that Little John and Robin Hood had played on him. He lamented to all and finally went to London to tell the King.

But the King said, "Why, Sheriff, what would you have me do? Aren't you my Sheriff? Isn't it your duty to deal with such outlaws? You have the power, you have the law, to help you crush that man. Invent some way to draw him and his crew into your town and then you can try to catch them all."

The Sheriff was spurred to think now and devised a luring game. All the archers in the north of England should come one day that autumn. Those who shot the best would take home prizes. He that shot the very best would win a silver arrow tipped with gold, the like of which did not exist in England.

When Robin Hood heard of this contest, he said, "Get ready, my men, for I am going to win."

Now Midge the miller's son had heard from

his father, who heard through a friend, who heard through one of the Sheriff's many men, that the purpose of this contest was to draw out Robin Hood and his men from the forest and into the town, and that, once there in Nottingham, the Sheriff and his men would shoot them down.

But Robin Hood was keen to have that prize arrow, and he turned his mind this way and that. "Listen to me, my men, my friends, my Midge, my Little John: come what may, I have to try my skill at that archery. But this shall we do. We shall not wear our Lincoln green cloaks. We shall dress so that the Sheriff's men will not find us. One shall wear white, another red, one yellow, one blue."

So out through the forest they went, all with steady hearts and minds. They mixed themselves with the people who came to Nottingham for the contest, and the Sheriff, who looked and looked for the Lincoln green cloaks that identified Robin Hood's men, saw none and was vexed. "I thought he would have been here," said the Sheriff, scratching his head. To the herd of contestants, he announced, "Though Robin Hood is brave, he's not so brave as to appear."

When Robin Hood, whose red cloak masked him, heard these words, he winced with pain. "Not brave! I, not brave?"

Standing beside the Sheriff on this day was his pretty fiancée. Christine was as bright and kind as the Sheriff was dark and mean. As they watched the contest he said to her, "If Robin Hood were here, and all of his men to boot, surely none of them could shoot better."

"That man in red," said Christine, "is clearly the best of all." And as she said this, Robin Hood, the man she meant, turned and smiled at the Sheriff. The Sheriff said, "Every shot you take is sure and on the spot. So the arrow with the golden head and the shaft of silver-white is yours, my friend. But tell me, archer, what is your name?"

"His name?" said the bishop, who had come to town to see the contest. The bishop was a man with a sharp eye for faces and remembered Robin's from Allen a Dale's wedding. "Robin Hood!" he exclaimed.

"Indeed it is," said Robin Hood. "You and the bishop were both once my guests. But remember, dear Sheriff, that not long ago, under the greenwood tree, we made a deal."

"Robin Hood!" said the Sheriff. "I hold to nothing said in a robber's nest. Men! My men, kill this thief!" And he himself would have run Robin Hood through with his sword, but his Christine, dear woman, checked his arm.

"Let him go, my darling," she said, "if you

ever gave him your word. A promise is a promise."

"No!" said the Sheriff. "A thief is a thief." He was angry, yet he held his arm and did not run Robin through.

"Woe to you, Sheriff," said Robin Hood, "for betraying your oath to me in the forest. Thank you, good lady, for reminding the Sheriff of his vow. But, Sheriff, will you let me and my men go, or shall I return your golden arrow to you in the chest and make your bright, good fiancée a widow before she is wed?" For Robin Hood had notched the golden arrow in his bow and had it aimed at his foe.

"I shall let you go," said the Sheriff. "I shall let you go—as far as the gates of Nottingham. Beyond those gates and within the forest, as you have made the King's deer your game, you and your men will be mine."

"Very well," said Robin Hood.

As soon as Robin and his men had left the town the Sheriff called together his men and his hounds. The Sheriff offered rewards to any man who killed a man of Robin Hood's, and a king's treasure to any who killed Robin Hood.

Now Robin Hood's men were hard sought after but managed their escape. Robin, however, was cut off in the forest by many Sheriff's men and dogs. He was like a deer, sensing danger on all sides. Unluckily, as he ran this way and that, a Sheriff's man saw him and shot an arrow that pierced his leg. Even so Robin managed to escape, and painfully crawled over the forest floor until he came near the castle of the man Robin had saved, Sir Richard. There, on the outskirts of the forest, Robin fell asleep with weariness, and in slumber's relief from pain he had a dream.

He dreamt of a woman. Her body was graceful, her body was straight, and her face free from pride. A bow was in her hand, and quiver and arrows hung dangling by her side. Her eyebrows were black and so was her hair, and her skin was as smooth as glass. Her face expressed wisdom and modesty too. Robin asked his dream vision, "Fair woman, where are you going?" And she answered, "To kill a fat buck, for tomorrow is a holiday." Robin said, "Fair woman, wander with me, down to the greenwood tree. You should sit down to rest." And as they were going toward the greenwood tree, they spied two hundred good bucks. She chose out the fattest in the herd and shot it through the side. "I swear," said Robin Hood, "I never saw a woman like you."

When he awoke, one of Sir Richard's men had found him and was carrying him from the edge of the forest and through the fields and into the castle, where Robin was put into a bed.

Sir Richard came to him and said, "I had heard that you won a contest and then were caught."

"Yes," said Robin Hood, gladly remembering his triumph. "I won the contest, but a Sheriff's archer then pierced my leg. I now beg of you a favor, my friend."

"I owe you favors forever," said Sir Richard. "You are hurt and I and my servants and my daughter will help you recover."

"That was just what I would ask. Thank you."

Now Marian was Sir Richard's daughter, and as beautiful as sunlight. When Robin Hood saw her, though he was almost faint with pain in his leg, the pain went to his heart, and he exclaimed to himself, "A Sheriff's man has shot my leg, but this goddess has shot my heart. I am in love. This is the woman of my dream."

Little John and Robin Hood's men were troubled and grieved that their master had disappeared, and they searched high and low for him and listened at the town walls for news, but no one, it seemed, had seen him. Robin Hood himself, who had never before

When Robin Hood saw her, the pain went to his
heart.

forgotten his men, forgot them now as Sir Richard's daughter helped nurse him back to health. But while his leg became well, his heart was still sore and tender.

"Sir Richard," said Robin one day. "I do not think I shall recover from my pain unless you grant me one favor more."

"Anything, my friend. You must be anxious for your friends. Let me send a messenger to them and tell them of your health."

"Tell them . . . that an archer has pierced my heart and that I shall never recover."

"But that is not true. It was your leg, and you are recovered nearly completely now."

"Sir Richard, please be generous to me. I ask you for your daughter's hand."

Never had Robin Hood seen his friend so confused, nor so sad. No, not even when the bishop was trying to turn Sir Richard out of his castle. Good Sir Richard staggered and sat down, and then said, "Forgive me, Robin. Forgive me, my friend. I did not expect this. My daughter, you say? My dearest? The comfort of my old age? The image of her mother, my departed wife?" He shook his head and wept.

"Sir Richard!"

"I would sooner give you my castle," said Sir Richard. "She is all I have."

"Then return, you yourself, with me and

Marian to the forest. My men and I are not knights, but we try to live well."

"Please let me consider," said Sir Richard. "My heart is stricken. I shall tell you tomorrow. I owe you almost everything, but it is my woe that you have chosen my daughter. And Marian, has she chosen you?"

"That is my heart's dream," said Robin. He was troubled also, because he did not know for certain that Marian was in love with him.

When the next day came, Sir Richard said to his daughter, "Marian, what would you have? Would you become the wife of our friend Robin Hood?"

"But if I married him," she said, "what would become of you, my father?"

"That is not the question," said the knight. Sir Richard called Robin Hood into the room, and now said again to Marian, "Would you become the wife of Robin?"

Marian bowed her head and closed her eyes, and said, "I will not, unless you, my father, live with us, wherever that might be."

"Six months," said Sir Richard, taking Marian's hand, "I will live with you and your husband, the good Robin Hood, in the forest. And six months will I live here alone. You shall marry Robin, my dear Marian."

And so Sir Richard consented to the wed-

ding between the hero and the hero's delight,
Marian. All of the merry men came to the ceremony, performed by Friar Tuck, and there
were celebrations and contests that lasted
many days. And then Sir Richard joined with
Robin's men and learned some of the skills of
the happy woodsmen, and he still enjoyed his
daughter's care and devotion, though it was
shared now between himself and Robin.

After six months, Sir Richard returned to
his castle, and was able to live almost happily
amongst his servants, because Marian would
visit regularly and because he had the happy
springtime to look forward to when he would
join again with Robin's merry men.

Robin Hood and the Potter

THE BIRDS were singing merrily, and there were blossoms on every tree, when one morning, in Sherwood Forest, Robin Hood and his men spied a cocky potmaker riding on his cart.

"Here comes that potter," said Robin Hood. "He's the one who has long used our trails and yet never has been kind enough to pay us a single penny for his toll."

"I met him once on the west-end bridge," said Little John. "He gave me three knocks so hard my sides still ache. I'll bet forty pieces of gold that there's not one of us who can make that potter pay us a toll."

"Here's the forty pieces," said Robin Hood. "I will make that potter pay." Robin Hood now rushed through the trees and stopped in the potter's way. Robin took the horse's bridle and ordered the potter to stop.

The angry potter said, "What do you want, outlaw?"

"For the last three years, you have traveled this way, and yet have never been kind enough to pay us a penny."

"Who are you," said the potter, "that you should ask me to pay a toll?"

"Robin Hood is my name, I am keeper of this forest, and a bag of gold is the fee."

"I will not pay you a cent. Now unhand my horse, or I'll beat you black and blue." The potter hopped off his seat, went to the back of his cart and pulled out a long staff. Robin pulled out a sword and his small round shield. The potter walked up toward Robin now and said, "Listen, my man, let my horse go."

Robin let go but set out to fight, and he with his sword and the potter with his staff went fiercely at it, like a dog and cat.

Robin's men were standing under their meeting tree and they laughed as they watched this battle. Little John said to his fellows, "That potter there will stand up to him." At that moment the potter knocked the shield out of Robin Hood's hand. Before Robin could pick up his shield, the potter clubbed him with his staff and Robin fell to the ground.

"Let's help our master," said Little John, "so the potter does not kill him." He and the other men went down to the trail where the potter stood over poor Robin.

Little John nodded to the potter, who took a step away, and Little John leaned over his master and tapped Robin on the shoulder.

"Who has won the bet, master? Shall you have my forty gold pieces, or shall I have yours?"

"What was mine, Little John," said Robin Hood, as dizzy as in a dream, "is now yours." And now Robin stood up.

"I have heard," said the potter, "that it is hardly courteous to stop a poor workingman and rob him of his goods."

"You speak the truth," said Robin. "You are a good man, and every day for ever more, you shall drive and never pay a toll. Indeed, dear potter, will you become my friend? Let me do your job today, and you shall do mine. Give me your clothes and I will give you mine, and I will go to Nottingham."

"I agree to that," said the potter. "And you shall find me a good friend to you. But how can you sell my pots for me, as you hardly know my trade?"

"I vow," said Robin, "I will take all your pots today to town, and return again with all of them sold." The potter and the outlaw changed their clothes, and the potter lay down under the tree.

But then spoke Little John, "Master, if you must go to Nottingham, take care to avoid the Sheriff, because as you know he is not our friend."

"The Sheriff will never know me. He will

take me for a potter," said Robin Hood, dab-
bing his face with clay. He left for Nottingham
to sell those pots, while the potter stayed with
Robin's men and enjoyed himself quite well.

When Robin Hood came to Nottingham, he
fed the horse some oats and hay. "Pots! Pots!"
he began to cry out. "The more you buy the
less you pay!"

In the middle of the town lived the Sheriff,
and Robin had parked his cart against the
Sheriff's front gate. Wives and widows surrounded Robin and quickly bought his pots.
Robin Hood continued to call out, "Pots, real
cheap! I would hate to stand here all day and
not sell all my pots! Pots! Pots, real cheap!
The more you buy the less you pay!"

The pots that were worth five pennies
Robin Hood sold for three. He sold two pots
for five, three for seven, five for ten. A man
and wife who watched him sell, said to each
other, "That potter is not too smart."

But in this way Robin Hood sold his pots
quite fast, till he had just five pots left. And
those five he took from off his cart and sent
up to the Sheriff's bride.

When Christine got those pots, she smiled
and laughed. "Oh, good potter," she called
from her window, "thank you. The next time
you come to Nottingham, I shall buy your pots
if I can."

"You will have only my best," said Robin.

"Kind potter," said Christine, "come dine with the Sheriff and me. That would truly make me glad."

"Because you ask," said Robin, "I shall accept." The Sheriff did not recognize Robin in his role as a potter, and gently and nicely asked Robin Hood into his house. The Sheriff's manners since marriage had greatly improved.

"Look, my dear," said Christine to her husband, "what the potter has given to you and to me. Five fine pots."

"You are generous, potter," said the Sheriff. "Let us wash up for dinner and then eat."

As they sat down at their meal, with pleasant and happy conversation, Robin Hood and the Sheriff overheard two of the Sheriff's men outside speak of a great big bet. "We shall have a contest of the bow and arrow," said one, "and bet forty gold pieces."

Robin loved all contests and was, of course, a master of the bow. The Sheriff and his wife watched him as he listened to the men, for he looked like a fox who has picked up a scent, his ears twitching and listening.

"May we watch your good men in their contest?" asked Robin Hood.

"For your entertainment, indeed," said the Sheriff.

The Sheriff gently and nicely asked Robin Hood
into his house.

He led his wife and Robin Hood out of doors to watch his men. But neither of the Sheriff's men shot very well at all. Robin itched to take a try and win for himself the gold. "If I had a bow," he said, "I bet that in one shot I could beat these men."

"You shall have a bow, then," said the Sheriff. "You shall have the choice of three." He sent his steward to retrieve his bows, and the best that the steward brought back was the one Robin chose. He weighed the bow, he looked along its edge, he studied it carefully.

"Now let's see if you are any good," said the Sheriff. "You seem to know your bows."

"Indeed," said Robin Hood, "this is very fine gear." Robin strung the bow as easily as a musician strings his lute. And now he went to the quiver of arrows and took out a good sharp shaft. He let the arrow fly and hit the target in the middle. The Sheriff's men shot again, and so did he. This time Robin again hit the very center, and split the wooden plug in three.

The Sheriff's men felt ashamed that the potter had won. The Sheriff laughed, clapped Robin on the back and said, "Potter, you are a real man. You are worthy to bear a bow anywhere you go."

"At home," said Robin, "I do have a bow, and it is the one that Robin Hood gave me."

"You know Robin Hood?" said the Sheriff. "Tell me how."

"I have shot with him a hundred times under his greenwood tree," said Robin Hood.

"I would rather have such a chance to stand beside that outlaw," said the Sheriff, "than to have a hundred pieces of gold."

"Then, if you take my advice," said Robin, "and will dare to go with me, tomorrow, before breakfast, we will see Robin Hood."

"I will repay you for this favor," said the Sheriff.

But when the Sheriff's wife Christine heard from her husband this plan, she said, "I am not as happy as you about this, dear. Robin Hood, you know, is a cunning thief. He shall not allow you, much less even our clever potter, to approach him by disguise."

"We shall see," said the Sheriff, unhappy with his wife's words.

As soon as it was morning, the Sheriff and Robin Hood got ready for the forest. Robin called goodbye to the Sheriff's wife and thanked her for her dinner. "My good lady," he said, bowing, "please accept this gold ring as a sign of my respect and good wishes to you."

"This is too much," said the good lady. "Five pots and now a ring!"

"No," said Robin Hood. "It is a trade for your kindness."

The Sheriff agreed and said, "Accept it, my dear, and I shall repay the potter when I am able."

"Then, thank you, potter, and may you get what you deserve," said the lady. The ring was very fine, and once had belonged to a lord who had paid his way out of Sherwood Forest with it.

The Sheriff rode along with Robin and was keen to meet his foe and arrest him. He peered this way and that, and Robin led him slowly. The leaves in the forest were green and bright, and birds were singing joyously among the boughs.

"It is delightful to be here," said Robin. "But I swear to you, if a man has a cent more than he needs, he will here meet Robin Hood." Robin put his horn to his mouth and blew a blast, and when his men heard it they started running through the woods. Little John came, reaching his master first, and said, "How have you done in Nottingham? Have you sold all your pots?"

"Yes, I certainly have," said Robin. "And see what I have brought in return, the Sheriff of Nottingham, as a prize for us all."

"He is quite welcome," said Little John. "This is good news."

The Sheriff, seeing that the potter was no potter, but Robin Hood, wished he had never left town. "If I had known, in Nottingham, that you were no potter but Robin Hood, I would not have let you return to the forest for a thousand years."

"I believe that," said Robin Hood. "And so I am pleased that you and I are here. And now that you are my guest, I must ask that you leave your horse with us, as well as all your other gear."

"I object to this robbery," said the Sheriff. "I will not allow it."

"But you must." And Robin's men surrounded the Sheriff and took from him all he had. "You came here," said Robin Hood, "on a horse to bring harm to me, my wife and my men, and home you shall go on foot. And when you get home, nicely greet your wife, because she is so very good—as you are not. Marian sends her a fine, white gentle horse. If not for the respect and gratitude I owe your wife, you would have more to suffer than that I take your goods."

And so Robin Hood told the Sheriff goodbye, and the Sheriff, leading the gentle white horse home to his wife, sadly went on his way to Nottingham.

"My dear," his wife Christine greeted him, "how was your journey into the forest? Have you brought the outlaw Robin Hood home to jail?"

"I curse that man, for Robin was the potter! I wish he were dead," said the Sheriff. "He has made me a fool! Everything I brought into that forest he has taken from me. I have nothing now but this white horse his wife has sent to you."

"Oh, my dear," said Christine, kissing his brow. "I see that you have paid for all the pots and the fancy ring Robin Hood gave to me. What he robbed from us he gave us back in trade."

Robin, meanwhile, was with his men and the potter under the greenwood tree drinking and eating and telling long stories. Finally, as evening set in, Robin asked, "Potter, what were your pots worth, the ones that I sold in Nottingham?"

"Altogether," said the potter, "two gold pieces."

"You shall have ten gold pieces for them," said Robin, paying out the money. "Thank you, and whenever you come back through Sherwood Forest, come visit us again."

Robin Hood and the Beggar

ONE DAY, while Marian was at the castle visiting her father, Sir Richard, Robin Hood was restless missing her, so he got upon his horse and set out riding toward Nottingham, looking for something to amuse him. On the outskirts of the town he saw a man.

The man was wearing an old, patched coat, and had several small sacks slung over his shoulders.

"Hello, hello," said Robin Hood. "Where are you from?"

"I am from Yorkshire, sir. But before you go on your way, will you please give me some charity?"

"Why, what would you like?" said Robin.

"No prayers, no advice," said the man, "but perhaps just a penny."

"I have no money," said Robin then. "I am a ranger of the forest. I am an outlaw, and my name is Robin Hood. But I ask you, my friend, that to change the pace, let's swap our clothes each for the other's. Your old coat for my green cloak. My horse for your bags."

"Very good, very good," said the man. "You offer more than you expect."

When Robin Hood had put on the man's clothes, he looked at himself and laughed. "I think I seem a big, brave beggar. And you," Robin said to the man, "you look quite dashing."

"Indeed, I will dash now, on this horse. And you, make use of those bags," said the man.

"I see," said Robin. "Now I have a bag for my bread, another for wheat, one for salt and one for my horn. And what shall I do with this empty one?"

"Go begging," said the man.

"Have you a penny?" asked Robin.

"Yes," said the man, "I have several, but I never give money to beggars." The man laughed and went on his way.

As Robin started on another way, with the bags hanging about him, and the man's long staff and the old patched coat, he felt as jolly as could be. Along the path, riding fine horses, came two tubby priests, all dressed in black.

"I beg you," said Robin Hood, "have pity on me. Please give me a penny, for our dear Lord's sake. I have been wandering all day, with nothing offered, and not so much as one little drink nor bit of bread to eat."

"Get out of the way," said one priest, a red-headed fellow. "Neither of us has a penny."

"Yes," said the other, a blond-bearded man. "Not a penny. This morning were we robbed."

"I am very much afraid," said Robin, "that you are both telling a lie. Before you ride on, I am resolved to find out the truth."

When the priests heard this beggar say that, they kicked at their horses, but Robin Hood took hold of the bridles. Then he reached up and pulled down the men and they spilled to the ground with a thud.

"Spare us, beggar," said the redheaded priest.

"Have pity," said the blond-bearded one.

"You said you have no money," said Robin. "Therefore, right now, we three will go to our knees, and pray as hard as we can for some gold."

The priests could not run, they could not fight, and so they went to their knees to do as the beggar told them. "Send us, O send us," they prayed aloud, "some money to serve our needs." After they had prayed for a few hours, Robin said, "Now let's see what money heaven has sent. We shall be sharers all alike of the money that we have."

The priests put their hands in their pockets but found no money at all.

"Let's search each other," said Robin. "One by one."

Then Robin took pains to search them both, and hidden within their cloaks, coats, hats and shoes, as if by miracle, he found a good sum of money. There were five hundred gold pieces, in fact, that he emptied upon the grass.

"This is amazing," said Robin, "to see such a vast amount. You have both prayed so well that you shall each have a part."

He gave them fifty coins apiece and kept the rest for himself. They got up to leave, but Robin Hood said no. "I have one more thing to say," said Robin. "I want you both to swear that you will never tell lies again, wherever you go, wherever you are. The other promise I want you to keep is this, that you shall be charitable to the poor. I am a holy beggar, and that is all I say."

The priests said they promised. Robin nodded, set them upon their horses once more and watched them ride away.

"What would Marian think of me?" wondered Robin Hood. "Have I done bad or good? I miss her and I am aimless. I shall venture now to Nottingham, and go to church."

Outside the church, he met a sobbing woman, and he said, "What is it, good lady? May I help you somehow?"

"You are a beggar, are you not?" she said, her eyes quite full of tears.

"I am, but I am sturdy. I am strong and I am good. I am at your service."

"Then rescue, please, my sons," the good lady said. "The Sheriff means to hang them for shooting the King's deer."

"The King's deer?" said Robin. This reminded Robin of when he was a young man, and was to be punished for just this crime in just this way. "The King's deer are mine."

"Are you the King?" asked the woman.

"No, but within Sherwood Forest, I am as good as one. My name is Robin Hood."

"Then, please, good Robin Hood, save my boys. They do no more harm than you do, and they only killed the deer so that I and their sisters could eat."

"I will save them, good lady, if it is up to me."

Robin, who looked to the Sheriff like a beggar, made his way to the gallows, where the Sheriff was preparing to hang the young men.

"Tell me, Sheriff," said Robin, "what did these men do?"

"They are robbers, as bad as Robin Hood," said the Sheriff. "They will receive what that outlaw should get."

"We shall see," said Robin. He now edged through the crowd that came to watch this horrible sight. But before the hangman could perform his work, Robin begged a long stick from a dog, and from a woman a piece of string, and from a boy three broken arrows. He still had his horn, and as the young men put their heads near the ropes that would hang them, Robin Hood strung his make-shift bow and fired his three arrows, cutting the ropes in two. He pulled out his horn and blew, and dodged the Sheriff's men, until Little John and Will and Allen and Arthur and the others came running, rescuing him and the boys.

The Sheriff retreated into his house, and his wife Christine said sadly, "I told you you should not try to hang young men. No good could come of that. They killed deer only because they needed food for their family's table."

"I hate Robin Hood," said the Sheriff.

"You ought to forgive him for helping you not make an error."

"Ought I to pardon him, too?"

"Perhaps," said his wife.

"I cannot do that," said the Sheriff.

"Then let us enjoy our supper, and thank our good fortune we have food enough," said Christine.

"That I may do," said the Sheriff. He admired his wife for her good sense and fine feeling, and resolved to pardon the hungry young men.

When Robin and his merry men returned to the forest, Marian was there awaiting him.

"I have shot you a deer, and brought you wine and beer," she said. "I hope you have missed me, my poor beggar man. You have done a fine deed for those young men, and I love you."

They kissed and hugged, and Robin's men laughed and cheered.

"Good master," said Little John. "We shall leave you in peace for the rest of the week. We are going hunting."

And so ends our tale of Robin Hood, who, with his jolly men and Marian, lived happily ever after under the greenwood tree in England's Sherwood Forest.